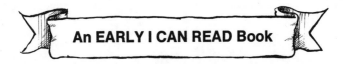

An EARLY I CAN READ Book

Weekly Reader Books presents

HATTIE RABBIT

by Dick Gackenbach

Harper & Row, Publishers
New York, Hagerstown, San Francisco, London

To Jim Giblin

This book is a presentation of Weekly Reader Books.
Weekly Reader Books offers book clubs for children from
preschool through high school.

For further information write to:
Weekly Reader Books
4343 Equity Drive
Columbus, Ohio 43228

HATTIE RABBIT

Library of Congress Catalog Card Number: 75-37018
Trade ISBN 0-06-021939-4
Harpercrest ISBN 0-06-021940-8

Wishes For Hattie

"Your mother has funny feet,"

said Hattie Rabbit to Little Chicken.

"They are good

for scratching up worms,"

said Little Chicken.

"I wish," said Hattie,

"my mother had feet like that."

4

"Your mother has a very long neck,"
said Hattie to Little Giraffe.
"She can reach the tender leaves
at the tops of trees,"
said Little Giraffe.
"I wish," said Hattie,
"my mother had a neck that long."

"That is some nose your mother has,"
said Hattie to Little Elephant.
"It is great for taking a bath,"
said Little Elephant.

Hattie watched Little Elephant

get his bath.

"Wow!" she said.

"I wish my mother

had a nose like that."

"Goodness," thought Hattie.

"What if my wishes came true?"

She thought some more.

"If my mother had feet

like Mrs. Chicken," she said,

"I would have to eat worms.

Ugh, I hate worms."

"If she had a neck

like Mrs. Giraffe,

I would have to climb

on a ladder

to give her a kiss."

13

"If she had a nose

like Mrs. Elephant,

one sneeze

would blow the roof

right off our house."

15

"No," said Hattie,

"I take my wishes back.

I want my mother

the way she is.

Warm,

soft,

and furry."

Open For Business

Hattie sold her friend Ronald

a glass of lemonade

for a nickel.

"Ugh, bla-a," said Ronald.

"That's awful!"

"I never said there was sugar in it,

did I?" said Hattie.

She put the nickel

in her purse.

Ronald would not talk to her

anymore.

Hattie sold her friend Mabel

a surprise package

for four cents.

"It is something

good and heavy,"

said Hattie.

Mabel opened the box.

It was full of rocks.

"You are terrible," said Mabel.

"I said it would be a surprise,"

said Hattie.

Mabel would not talk to her

anymore.

"How would you like

a sandwich for fifteen cents?"

Hattie asked her friend Donald.

Donald was very hungry.

"Okay," he said.

Hattie handed Donald

a witch she had made

out of wet sand.

"You are crummy," said Donald.

"I told you it was a Sand Witch,"

said Hattie.

Now Donald would not talk to her

anymore.

"I will tell you a big secret

for a penny,"

said Hattie to her friend Marie.

"All right," said Marie.

Hattie put the penny in her purse.

"Now what is the big secret?"

asked Marie.

"The moon is made of margarine

and not real butter,"

Hattie whispered.

"You just made that stupid secret up,"

said Marie.

Marie was mad at Hattie, too.

Hattie counted her money.

She had twenty-five cents.

But she had no one

to play with.

What good was

the twenty-five cents?

Hattie went to the candy store

and bought lots of

Peanut Brittle.

She spent

all her money.

Hattie gave some Peanut Brittle

to Ronald,

some to Donald,

some to Mabel,

and the rest to Marie.

Hattie did not have

twenty-five cents

anymore.

But

she had all

her good friends back again.